I Can't Wait!

By
Samantha Young

Illustrations by Floyd Yamyamin

AuthorHouse™
1663 Liberty Drive
Bloomington, IN 47403
www.authorhouse.com
Phone: 833-262-8899

Because of the dynamic nature of the Internet, any web addresses or links contained in this book may have changed since publication and may no longer be valid. The views expressed in this work are solely those of the author and do not necessarily reflect the views of the publisher, and the publisher hereby disclaims any responsibility for them.

This book is printed on acid-free paper.

ISBN: 978-1-4772-6013-5 (sc)
ISBN: 978-1-4772-6021-0 (e)

Library of Congress Control Number: 2012915350

Print information available on the last page.

Published by AuthorHouse 07/20/2022

authorHOUSE®

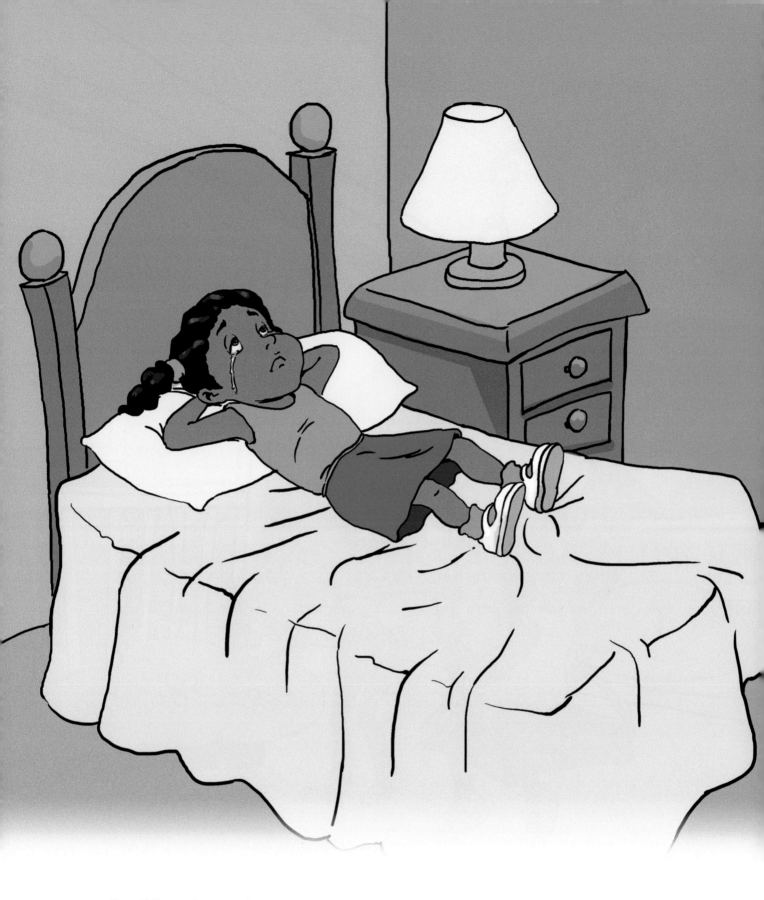

On Monday I feel blue, because I'm missing you.

On Tuesday I try not to have a fit, so I'll patiently sit.

On Wednesday I feel better, because I started writing
you a letter.

On Thursday I will cheer, for that time is almost near.

On Friday mommy cries because she's in for a big surprise.

On Saturday when I wake I'm going to bake him his favorite cake.

On Sunday is the day, a very special day, because this is the day my dad comes home to stay.

Uh oh! There he is!
We finally see him at last!
Yes! This day is going to be a blast!

I Love You Daddy!